THEATERGOER'S GUIDE

A McGRAW-HILL HANDBOOK FOR STUDENTS

Alvin Goldfarb
Scott Walters
Illinois State University

Edwin Wilson
Graduate School and University Center
The City University of New York

McGRAW-HILL, INC.

New York   St. Louis   San Francisco   Auckland   Bogotá   Caracas
Lisbon   London   Madrid   Mexico City   Milan   Montreal   New
Delhi   San Juan   Singapore   Sydney   Tokyo   Toronto

THEATERGOER'S GUIDE
A McGRAW-HILL HANDBOOK FOR STUDENTS

 This book is printed on recycled paper containing a minimum of 50%
total recycled fiber with 10% postconsumer de-inked fiber.

890 BKM BKM 9098

ISBN 0-07-070687-5

This handbook was set in Garamond.
The editors were Judith R. Cornwell and Susan Gamer.
The production supervisor was Terry Pace.
Book-mart Press, Inc., was printer and binder.

ACKNOWLEDGMENTS
Edwin Wilson's review of *Medea* (April 13, 1994) is reprinted with permission
of *The Wall Street Journal,* © 1994, Dow Jones and Company, Inc.; all rights
reserved.
Excerpts from *Playbill* by permission of PLAYBILL®. PLAYBILL® is a
registered trademark of PLAYBILL Incoporated, New York.
Excerpts from the program of *Sweeney Todd: The Demon Barber of Fleet
Street* printed by permission of Illinois State University Theatre Department.
John Sipes's program note for the *Macbeth Project* printed with permission of
the author.
Bethany E. Cottrell's review of *Sweeney Todd* printed by permission of the
author.

A very effective way to learn about theater is to attend and report on a performance: to see a play brought to life in a production complete with actors, sets, costumes, lights, sound, and audience—and then to describe your experience in the form of a written report. This *Theatergoer's Guide* (which accompanies *The Theater Experience* by Edwin Wilson and *Living Theater: A History, Theater: The Lively Art,* and *Theater: The Lively Art,* Brief Edition, by Edwin Wilson and Alvin Goldfarb) has been designed to help you enjoy your experience at the theater, appreciate it, and then write effectively about it.

THEATERGOING

Why Go to the Theater?

Why go to the theater at all? What is so special about a theater performance? In a theatrical performance, there are live performers in the presence of a live audience, and the electricity generated between actors and spectators is the most exciting aspect of attending a theater production. In theater—unlike film or television—each performance is unique because each audience responds differently and brings different expectations and sensibilities to the event. For example, think about a comedy onstage and a comedy in the movies. During the staged performance, the audience's response or lack of response will clearly affect the way the actors and actresses shape their performances; but during the running of the film, the reaction of the audience in the movie house can obviously have no impact on the performers. A theater event exists in time and changes over time; a film exists on celluloid and does not change. Remember, then, that although a theater performance has many components—including playing space, scenery, costumes, lighting, sound, and text—its primary elements are always the performers and the audience.

When people think about why they go to the theater, there are usually three basic reasons: entertainment, communal interaction, and personal growth. To begin with, for most audience members the desire to go to the theater is connected with their desire to be *entertained*. For these people, theater is a way to relax, a source of enjoyment and fun, an escape from daily existence. Slapstick comedies, farces, musicals, and melodramas are examples of theatrical works which are meant primarily to entertain. Second, a theatrical performance is a *communal experience:* it brings audience members together for a period of time. (In fact, the origins of theater are closely related to religious ceremonies and rituals, which are also communal experiences.) Third, theater can *enrich* individual audience members intellectually, emotionally, and perhaps spiritually; it can help us to see and understand the complexities and crosscurrents of everyday life and can also expand our horizons far beyond everyday life. Indeed, some theater artists believe that the function of theater is to "teach."

When you yourself attend the theater, try to determine your own reasons—keeping in mind that many theater pieces are both entertaining and enriching. From reading plays, watching television, and attending movies, you have probably formed a good idea of what kind of live theater you will enjoy. You know that comedies and farces can make you laugh and feel carefree. Dramas and tragedies can introduce you to new ways of looking at the world, and perhaps can lead you to think about parallels between your own experience and the universal human condition.

Preparing for Theatergoing

Before you attend a theater performance, you can do some preparation that will help you get the most out of it. Reading about the play you are going to see can add to your enjoyment and understanding. If the play is a classic, you might find some useful information about it in your textbook or a theater history book. In addition, there may be books or articles about the life and work of the playwright, or about drama and theater in the period when the play was written. You may also want to read the play itself. All this can provide background for you as a theatergoer.

Another effective way to prepare for a theater event is to read a review of the production. (A sample review is shown on the opposite page.) Often, you will find that a local newspaper has printed an article by a critic describing and evaluating the performance and giving background information about the play and playwright. A word of warning, however: do not be unduly swayed by the opinions expressed by the reviewer, since what you like may be completely different from what he or she prefers. Use the review only as a source of information, and go to the theater with an open mind.

A theater review

Greek Tragedy That Works

By Edwin Wilson

New York

Despite the fact that Greek tragedy is the fountainhead from which Western theater springs, it remains the most difficult form of drama to recreate in our own day. Greek plays employ a chorus for which we have no modern equivalent; they invariably contain long speeches describing events that take place offstage; and then there is all that raw emotion which can easily become too melodramatic. When, therefore, someone finds a way to transmit the power of a Greek play to a modern audience, it is a major accomplishment.

Director Jonathan Kent's new production of Euripides's "Medea" not only achieves that goal, it is exciting theater on its own terms. "Medea" is one of the most awesome and frightening tragedies ever

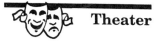 **Theater**

Jonathan Kent's "Medea"

written. In her native land, Medea betrayed her own family and killed her brother in order to save Jason, her husband. When Jason, having brought her to his home in Corinth, abandons her to marry the king's daughter, Medea, furious and hellbent on revenge, is ordered into exile with her two young sons.

She sends a magical robe to Jason's new bride which engulfs her in flames, and then, to plunge the knife of retribution deeper into the heart of Jason, she kills their sons. Along the way she makes impassioned speeches about the plight of women and their mistreatment in male-dominated societies.

The current production began at the small Almeida Theatre in North London, moved to the West End, and has now opened at the Longacre Theatre. In mounting the play, Mr. Kent made several key decisions, all of them inspired. The setting created by scene designer Peter J. Davison and lighting designer Wayne Dowdeswell is the corner of a courtyard: a three-story structure of huge, metal panels. When sections open and close, or characters strike the panels, they reverberate with a frightening, ear-splitting clang. The message is clear: Fearsome events are being hammered out within these walls.

Mr. Kent uses the set to excellent effect. Traditionally the primal screams and first words of Medea are uttered offstage: she is heard but not seen. Here, Medea is revealed in a panel on an upper level, seated in a chair, her face turned from the audience as she speaks. In other words, her physical presence is felt from the beginning.

In the scene where Medea is agonizing over whether or not to carry through her infanticide, a harsh, triangular beam of light slashes across the stage, pinning her in a corner. At the climax of the play, after Medea has murdered her sons inside her palace, three enormous metal panels break loose, falling with a clangor that lifts spectators from their seats.

Mr. Kent has also extracted maximum impact from his chorus, three ladies of Corinth (Judith Paris, Jane Loretta Lowe, and Nuala Willis) dressed in black Greek peasant outfits who chant and speak Jonathan Dove's score, sometimes in harmony, sometimes with a single voice. Their admonitions to Medea are counterpoint, relief, and agonizing prophecy of the black deeds to come. It is the most impressive use of a Greek chorus I can remember.

None of this would work, though, without a transcendent actress in the role of Medea, and here Mr. Kent has triumphed with Diana Rigg. She has an incredible vocal range, moving from the rich deep resonance of a cello or viola, to the insistent high peal of an oboe. One moment she unleashes fearsome cries and the next she colors a humorous exchange with deadly irony. Along with her vocal prowess is her presence and bearing. Always marked by dignity, intelligence and style, Ms. Rigg moves like quicksilver from one emotion to another but always with an unmistakable resolve. Her Medea is not a mindless barbarian but rather someone who knows exactly what she is doing. She agonizes over her course of action, but once she has made her decision, moves relentlessly toward her goal. This makes the outcome that much more awesome and appalling.

The new translation by Alistair Elliot is modern and accessible without being colloquial. The excellent cast performing with Ms. Rigg has been imported in toto from London. For 85 minutes without break, this is one of those rare experiences when a work of art from the past becomes a painful reminder of the fearful forces swirling around us today.

3

Buying Tickets

Buying tickets for a theater event can be done in many ways, depending on the type of theater you are attending. For example, if you want to see a large-scale commercial production on Broadway or in a major touring house, you can buy tickets through the box office, by telephone, or through a ticket agency. The best seats at such a production can cost as much as $75 each, but reduced-price tickets are often available: in many cities, there are special booths selling tickets at half price; student "rush" tickets are usually available on the day of the performance (sometimes just before the performance starts); and reduced-rate coupons may be offered (in New York these coupons are called *twofers*—originally, "two for" the price of one).

If you are going to a small theater or a noncommercial theater, you may find that tickets can be bought only at the box office, and sometimes only on the day of the performance. (This is true, for example, at some off-off-Broadway theaters in New York.)

It is difficult to generalize about regional theaters, since there is a wide variety of such theaters across the United States, each with its own method of selling tickets. To buy tickets for a performance at a regional theater, the best thing to do is to call the box office for information, or look at a local newspaper to find an advertisement for the play.

Traditional pasteboard theater tickets still exist, though today tickets are often generated and printed out by computer. If seating is reserved, your ticket will tell you where you are seated. "General admission" tickets, on the other hand, do not entitle you to a specific seat, so you might want to arrive at the theater early to be sure of getting a good location. (If you have a reserved seat, you should be sure to arrive on time, since many theaters will not seat latecomers until there is an appropriate break in the performance.)

The Lobby

The lobby of a theater space is a "holding area" for the audience members before they enter the auditorium. Usually, a lobby tells you something about what kind of theater experience you can expect to have. For example, commercial Broadway theaters, well-established regional theaters, and touring houses often have lavish lobbies; off-Broadway, off-off-Broadway, and alternative theaters frequently have small lobbies that are modestly decorated or even undecorated. In some small theaters, there may be no lobby at all: the audience members simply congregate out on the street.

You may find considerable information in the lobby which can help you better understand and appreciate a theater event. For example, there may be photographs of the performers and other artistic personnel (these photos are known as *head shots),* photos of the current production or past productions, posters reflecting the point of view of the production, historical information about the theater or the company, or awards won by the company. In addition, you might be able to pick up brochures for season tickets or future productions.

From the moment you enter the lobby area, you should begin to assess your feelings about the experience.

Programs

As you enter the auditorium, you will probably receive a program from an usher who may also escort you to your seat. The program will contain much useful information that can help you enjoy and understand the theater event.

In the program, you will find the title of the play, the author, the cast of characters, the actors and actresses, the designers, the director, and various other people involved in mounting the production. In some playbills, you will also find brief biographies of these people. In addition, you will find information about the setting of the play (place and time), its division into acts or scenes, and the number of intermissions. (Examples from programs for a Broadway production and a university production are shown on the following pages.)

Some playbills also include notes about the play; such notes may be written by the playwright, the director, or the dramaturg—the literary advisor to the production. (An example of such a note is shown on page 10.) Notes like these can make you aware of the historical relevance of a play and the director's approach to the text.

Be sure to read the program and any notes in it, but don't read this material during the actual course of the performance. The best time to read the program is either before the performance starts or during intermissions.

OPENING NIGHT: JANUARY 14, 1993

CRITERION CENTER STAGE RIGHT

TODO HAIMES, Artistic Director
presents

| LIAM | NATASHA | RIP |
| NEESON | RICHARDSON | TORN |

in

ANNA CHRISTIE

by

EUGENE O'NEILL

Also Starring
ANNE MEARA

with

| BARTON | CHRISTOPHER |
| TINAPP | WYNKOOP |

Directed by
DAVID LEVEAUX

Set Design by	*Costume Design by*	*Lighting Design by*
JOHN LEE	**MARTIN**	**MARC B.**
BEATTY	**PAKLEDINAZ**	**WEISS**
Composer & Sound Designer	*Fight Director*	*Production Stage Manager*
DOUGLAS J.	**STEVE**	**KATHY J.**
CUOMO	**RANKIN**	**FAUL**
Casting by		*General Manager*
PAT McCORKLE/		**ELLEN RICHARD**
RICHARD COLE, C.S.A.		

Founding Director
GENE FEIST

Roundabout Theatre Company productions are made possible, in part, with public funds
from the National Endowment for the Arts, Natural Heritage Trust, the New York State
Council on the Arts and the New York City Department of Cultural Affairs.
The Education Program is made possible, in part, by a generous grant from
BankAmerica Foundation.
Roundabout Theatre Company gratefully acknowledges Johnnie Walker Black Label's
sponsorship of the 1992-93 Singles Series.
Roundabout Theatre Company is a member of the League of American Theatres
and Producers, Inc.

WHO'S WHO IN THE CAST

LIAM NEESON (*Mat Burke*). Stage credits include seasons at Belfast's Lyric Theatre; *Dr. Fell, Death of Humpty Dumpty* and *Of Mice and Men* at Dublin's Abbey Theatre; *The Informer, Streamers* and *Says I, Says He* at the Dublin Theatre Festival; *One Flew Over the Cuckoo's Nest* at Dublin's Gaiety Theatre; *Translations* at Britain's National Theatre; and *The Plough and the Stars* at the Royal Exchange Theatre, Manchester. Neeson's numerous film roles include the current *Leap of Faith* and *Husbands and Wives*, as well as *Excalibur, The Bounty, Lamb, Duet for One, A Prayer for the Dying, The Mission, Suspect, High Spirits, The Good Mother, The Dead Pool, Darkman, Crossing the Line, Shining Through* and *Under Suspicion*. He will also star in the title role of "Ethan Frome" for American Playhouse. His television work includes "If Tomorrow Comes," "A Woman of Substance," "Hold the Dream," "Sworn to Silence," "Ellis Island" and "Sweet As You Are." This marks Liam Neeson's Broadway debut.

NATASHA RICHARDSON (*Anna Christopherson*) trained at the Central School of Speech and Drama in England. Her professional acting career began in regional theatre. She then appeared in London in a number of productions, including *A Midsummer Night's Dream,* in which she played Helena, and in *Hamlet* as Ophelia. Her performance as Nina in *The Seagull* won her the London Drama Critics Poll for Most Promising Newcomer of 1986. Her other stage performances include Tracy Lord in *High Society* and Anna Christie in the Young Vic Theatre production. Richardson's feature films include *Gothic; Patty Hearst; A Month in the Country; Fat Man and Little Boy; The Favour, the Watch, and the Very Big Fish; The Handmaid's Tale;* and *The Comfort of Strangers* (for which she won the London Evening Standard Award for Best Actress of 1990). Richardson most recently completed the BBC motion picture of the Tennessee Williams play *Suddenly Last Summer,* also starring Maggie Smith and Rob Lowe, directed by Richard Eyre. Miss Richardson, who lives in NYC, is making her Broadway debut in this production.

RIP TORN (*Chris Christopherson*). Conceived in Manhattan, born in Texas, he was named after his late father, Elmore Torn, from whom he received the family moniker "Rip," which he shares with his Uncle Roland and his cousin, Sam (this vouched for by his mother, Thelma). His six children and two grandchildren were born in this city. He now lives in Connecticut. Plays: *Cat on a Hot Tin Roof, Sweet Bird of Youth* (Theatre World Award), *The Glass Menagerie, Strange Interlude, Desire Under*

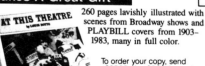

SWEENEY TODD
The Demon Barber of Fleet Street
A Musical Thriller

Music and Lyrics by   Book by
STEPHEN SONDHEIM   HUGH WHEELER

From an Adaptation by
CHRISTOPHER BOND

Originally Directed by HAROLD PRINCE
Originally Produced on Broadway by Richard Barr,
Charles Woodward, Robert Fryer, Mary Lea Johnson, Martin Richards
in Association with Dean and Judy Manos

Director . . . . Calvin MacLean
Music Director and Conductor . . . . Glenn Block
Co-Conductor . . . . Julian Dawson
Choreographer . . . . Connie de Veer
Scenic Designer . . . . John C. Stark, U.S.A.A.
Lighting Designer . . . . Shawn Malott *
Costume Designer . . . . Susan L. Hayes
Sound Designer . . . . Jon Kusner
Technical Director . . . . Dan Browder
Stage Manager . . . . Christina Saylor

*MFA Candidate

SETTING

1850's London

—There will be one 15-minute intermission—

CAST

in order of appearance

Sweeney Todd . . . . Brian Herriott
Anthony Hope . . . . Dave Vish
Beggar Woman . . . . Carolyn Brady
Mrs. Lovett . . . . Anita B. Deely
The Birdseller . . . . Aaron M. Shelton
Johanna . . . . Susan Lewis
Judge Turpin . . . . Joe Greene
Beadle Bamford . . . . David Zarbock
Tobias Ragg . . . . Dwight Powell
Adolfo Pirelli . . . . Andrew Kott
A Young Girl . . . . Anna Adams Stark
Jonas Fogg . . . . John W. Davis

Ensemble:

Rebecca Cooper	Aldo LaPietra	Richard Repp
John W. Davis	Kevin MacLean	Rob Scharlow
Gwendolyn Druyor	Sarah Manley	Aaron M. Shelton
Cindy Hinners	Katie Maringer	Regina Siciliani
	Jerry Myers	Kathy Taylor

ISU Opera Orchestra

Glenn Block, Music Director & Conductor
Julian Dawson, Co-Conductor
Kevin Medows, Assistant Conductor

VIOLIN
Rebecca Mertz, concertmaster
Carlene Easley
Andrew Guinzio
Deborah Paulsen
Melissa Shilling

VIOLA
Jon Feller, principal
Amy Govert

CELLO
Bo Li, principal
Maria Cooper
Jenny Holtman
Rebecca Pokarney

BASS
Joshua Harms, co-principal
Clifford Hunt, co-principal

FLUTE
Colleen McCoy, co-principal
Kristie Skinner, co-principal

OBOE/ENGLISH HORN
Andrea Imre, principal
Jeannie Ohnemus,
english horn

CLARINET
Jamian Green, principal
Traci Typlin
Karl Kalis, bass clarinet

BASSOON
Douglas Milliken
Christopher Harrison

REEDS
Jeffery Womack

HORN
Brandon Sinnock, co-principal
Kent Baker, co-principal

TRUMPET
Troy McKay, principal
Dan Forster
Deborah Whitfield
Modena Paulsen

TROMBONE
Charlie Plummer, principal
Steven A. Fox
Dawn Trotter, bass
trombone

TIMPANI
Nancy Rogers

PERCUSSION
Timothy Ryan, principal
Michael Mercer

KEYBOARD
Kevin Medows

STAFF
Kevin Medows, Assistant
Conductor
Carlene Easley, Manager/
Librarian

CHORAL DIRECTOR
Alejandro Rutty

REHEARSAL PIANISTS
Mária Horvath
Kevin Medows
Nancy Porter

THE MACBETH PROJECT

The Macbeth Project was conceived as an experiment in terms of both process and product. In principle, the rehearsal process was to include the collaborative efforts of all the participants, moving freely across lines of specialization and responsibility. William Shakespeare's Macbeth was chosen as the source of inspiration, both to focus experimentation and to stimulate the individual voices of the group. During the course of the rehearsal period, the company explored many dimensions of Shakespeare's play and experimented with ways to express aspects of the play which engaged the group's sensibilities. There was not, however, a self-imposed obligation placed upon the group to present a production of Macbeth. The group had the option to remain as close to Shakespeare's play or range as far from it as was necessary to allow their point of view to evolve and take shape. The final "product" of the project was not envisioned at the beginning of the process.

The Theater Environment

The *environment* of a theater event has several aspects, and these will affect your experience.

One of the most important elements you will encounter when you enter a theater is the performance *space*. The presentation may be taking place in a traditional theater building with an arena, thrust, or proscenium stage; in a converted space; or in a "found" space.

Another aspect of the environment is the *locale* of the theater. Theater spaces are found in many different locales. For example, New York has theaters in the Broadway district, off-Broadway, and off-off-Broadway. For the most part, Broadway theaters are large proscenium-arch spaces; off-Broadway theaters (as the term implies) are outside the Broadway district, are much smaller, and usually seat about 300 in a proscenium, thrust, or arena configuration; off-off-Broadway theaters house experimental groups in small found spaces and seat only about 100.

Across the United States, the many regional theaters have a variety of shapes and sizes. Larger cities often have alternative theaters, which are like the off-Broadway and off-off-Broadway theaters in New York. Commercial road-show houses are modeled after Broadway theaters. Some theater spaces outside of New York are much larger than Broadway theaters: there are municipal auditoriums and opera houses seating as many as 3,000 to 4,000.

Other types of theater environments include dinner theaters, which combine theatrical entertainment with dining and are very popular in many cities—for example, Orlando, Florida. Many communities have popular amateur community theaters, housed in traditional theater spaces or found spaces. High schools, colleges, and universities also produce many theatrical events for their own students and their communities.

Each theater environment creates a specific ambience and unique expectations on the part of the audience. As you enter a theater and its playing space, you might want to think about what the atmosphere is like and what impact it has on you. After you are seated, but before the performance actually begins, you may also want to think about, and assess, certain other elements. Is there a curtain, for example? If so, is it raised or lowered? What effect does a raised or lowered curtain suggest? If the curtain is up, is scenery visible? If so, what does the scenery seem to suggest about the production?

Audience Etiquette

Western theater, particularly since the nineteenth century, has developed certain rules of behavior for audience members—expectations about what audiences do and don't do. However, you should keep in mind that any given theater event might have some unique expectations about the audience's behavior.

At a traditional theater performance, the audience is expected to remain silent for the most part, and not to interrupt the performers. Audience members should not talk to each other as if they were at home watching television; they should not hum or sing along with music, unwrap candy or other food, eat loudly, search through a purse or backpack, or take notes in a distracting way; they should also shut off wristwatch alarms and beepers. Remember that the actors can hear the audience: noises and distracting behavior will have an impact on their concentration and performance. Noise and distractions also affect the experience of other spectators.

Students may be concerned about note-taking, since they often will need to make notes in order to remember key elements of the production. An unobtrusive way of taking notes is to jot down only brief phrases or terms which will jog your memory later. Then, you can embellish your notes during the intermission or intermissions, or after the last curtain.

Of course, traditional audiences are not always absolutely quiet: audiences at comedies can laugh, for instance. Audiences at musicals can applaud after a song (in fact, they're expected to). On the other hand, audiences at serious plays might not applaud until the end of the performance—and even then, an audience may be so stunned or so deeply moved that there will be a moment of silence before the applause begins.

As noted above, not all of these traditional expectations may apply at every theater event. Dinner theaters are one example, since the audience may be eating during the presentation. (We might also note that audiences eat during the performance in many traditional Asian theaters, and they may speak back to the stage.) Audiences at some productions are expected to interact with the performers: in some comic presentations, for instance, actors may enter the audience space or actually speak to individual audience members; and in some nontraditional productions, audience members may even be expected to participate in the performance. (We should mention, however, that because this kind of interaction or participation departs from the usual behavior of theater audiences, it makes some theatergoers feel uncomfortable.)

Intermissions

Intermissions serve a variety of functions. Of course, you do not have to leave your seat: many audience members stay in place and use the time just to stand and stretch. You can, however, use the respite to review your notes, go to the restroom, buy refreshments (if they are available), and discuss the production with friends. In most theaters, smoking in the lobby is no longer allowed, so smokers must go outside. You'll need to keep your ticket stub if you leave the lobby area.

An intermission usually lasts about 15 minutes, and the lights in the lobby will be flashed on and off as a signal that the intermission is ending. You should return to your place when signaled to do so, because the theater may not seat you if you return late, after the performance has resumed.

Keeping an Open Mind

One of the main purposes of theater is to let you see the world from different perspectives and experience differing viewpoints and lifestyles. Consequently, there may be times when what you see onstage will be something you disagree with or even find offensive. In a situation like this, it is helpful to keep an open mind while you are watching the performance. It is not necessary for you to agree with or approve of what you are hearing or seeing, and you may find that after the show is over you reject everything that has been presented. However, while the performance is going on, you should try to suspend judgment and experience it as receptively and tolerantly as possible.

HOW TO WRITE A THEATER REPORT

In this section, we'll give you some guidelines for writing a report on a theater event. But the first and most important advice we can give you is this: be sure not to let concerns (or even fears) about writing a paper prevent you from fully enjoying the theater experience itself. You should not become so distracted by note-taking, for example, that you cannot concentrate carefully on what is taking place in the performance. Your response to a production will be determined by how closely you have been engaged by the action onstage. If you spend too much time and effort thinking about your report during the performance, you will defeat the purpose of attending the theater.

Turning Notes into a Report

You should expand your notes into a complete report as soon as possible, while your impressions are still fresh; many instructors recommend writing a report the same day as the performance or no later than a day or two after it. The longer you wait, the harder it will be to reconstruct your experience and substantiate your impressions by citing specific examples and instances. (Keep in mind that most theater critics are expected to respond almost instantaneously to performances they see; in a sense, you too are being asked to make quick critical judgments.)

It is useful to begin with an outline and then write a draft based on your outline. To prepare your outline and draft, consider using the questions on pages 16–19 and the worksheets on pages 20–24. Next, revise your draft as often as necessary to produce the final report. As you revise, check your spelling and grammar carefully. Although theater courses are not English courses, all instructors expect papers that have been thoroughly edited and proofread. In addition, although it is your ideas which will earn most of the grade, a sloppily constructed paper will not present your ideas well.

What Makes a Good Theater Report?

A good theater report depends on content (what's in the paper), structure (how the paper is organized), and usage (conventions of writing and presentation). A sample report—with comments and corrections by an instructor—is shown at the end of this handbook.

Content A good theater report is a combination of subjective responses—how you "felt" about the event—and objective analysis and support for your feelings. Just saying that you liked or disliked a production is not enough. The key question is always "Why?" For example, you may have hated a performer in a production, but noting that you hated him or her is not enough for a report. *Why* did you feel this way? Was the actor totally unlike the character? Did the actor fail to enunciate the lines clearly? Did the actor convey emotions that seemed inappropriate to the dramatic action? Did he or she move inappropriately or clumsily onstage? Did he or she seem not to understand or express the character's motivation? These are the kinds of questions you will need to answer in order to substantiate your opinion about the performance, and you will have to support each answer by describing some specific aspect of the performance.

14

This is where your notes can be of great value. The more specific your notes, the more useful they are. Below, we suggest a series of questions about each production element. You can use these questions to guide your note-taking.

Structure   Like a good play, a good theater report has a clear beginning, middle, and end.

At the *beginning,* you should state your point of view; you may also indicate how you felt about the production in general or about the specific elements you will discuss. Sometimes a good paper can begin with a striking image or an idea which you believe to be at the heart of the theatergoing experience. The most important characteristic of the beginning of a successful paper is that it gives a strong sense of what you consider significant about your experience.

The *middle* of your paper should contain all the evidence and analysis that substantiates the viewpoint expressed in the beginning. This would include specific examples and details from the production. The more specific and analytical this section is, the more successful the paper will be. Through your description and analysis, the reader should be able to visualize important and representative moments in the production.

At the *end* of your paper, you should recapitulate your point of view and find some way to leave the reader with a clear sense of the conclusions you have drawn. As with the beginning of a paper, it can be effective to close the paper with a vivid image or idea. Remember that your conclusion will be the last impression left with your reader.

Usage   There are a few conventions for writing about theater productions. For example, the title of a play is usually capitalized; and the title of a full-length play is either underlined or italicized, though the title of a one-act play is generally in quotation marks. When you name production personnel, the first reference should give the full name, but thereafter only the last name should be used.

Most instructors expect papers to be typed or printed out rather than handwritten. If you use a personal computer, remember that the "spell check" will not catch every error: you cannot rely on it for names, for example, and of course it does not pick up grammatical mistakes. Remember too that word processing requires careful attention to formatting and printing. The harder it is for your instructor to read your paper, the harder it will be for him or her to evaluate your ideas.

Your instructor may recommend or require specific stylistic rules or a specific physical format for papers. Be sure that you understand such requirements at the beginning of the semester.

Key Questions for a Theater Report

These questions are intended as a guide for writing a theater report. You can use them to help you focus your thoughts about the various elements of a production. Note that you should keep the specific assignment in mind, since some instructors will ask you to write about particular elements whereas others may ask you to evaluate the entire production. In either case, however, these questions should prove helpful.

Acting

1. Were the actors believable, given the requirements of the play? If they were believable, how did they seem to accomplish this? If they weren't believable, what occurred to impair or destroy believability? (As you discuss this, be sure to separate the performer from the *role*. For example, you can dislike a character but admire the performance.)

2. Identify the performers you considered most successful. Citing specifics from the production, note what they did well: particular gestures, lines, or moments. Try to describe each performer so as to give the reader a clear image. For example, how did the performer's voice sound? How did he or she move? How did he or she interpret the role?

3. If there were performers you did *not* like, identify them and explain why you did not like them. Give concrete examples to explain why their performances were less successful.

4. Acting is more than just a collection of individual performances. The entire company needs to work as a unit (this is sometimes called *ensemble):* each actor must not only perform his or her own role but also support the other performers. Discuss how the performers related or failed to relate to one another. Did they listen to each other and respond? Did any actor seem to be "showing off" and ignoring the others?

Directing

1. The director unifies a production and frequently provides an interpretation of the text. Did there seem to be a unifying idea behind the production? If so, how would you express it? How were you able to see it embodied in the production? Was it embodied in striking images or in the way the actors developed their performances? (You should be aware that this can be one of the most difficult aspects of a production to evaluate, even for very experienced theatergoers.)

2. Did all the elements of the production seem to be unified and to fit together seamlessly? How was this reflected, in particular, in the visual elements—the scenery, costumes, and lighting?

3. How did the director move the actors around onstage? Were there any moments when you felt that such movement was particularly effective or ineffective? Were entrances and exits smooth?

4. Did the pace or rhythm of the production seem right? Did it drag or move swiftly? Did one scene follow another quickly, or were there long pauses or interruptions?

Space

1. What type of theater was it? How large or small was it? How opulent or elaborate? How simple or modern? What type of stage did it have: proscenium, thrust, arena, or some other type? How did the stage space relate to audience seating?

2. What was the size and shape of the playing space?

3. What sort of atmosphere did the space suggest? How was that atmosphere created?

4. Did the space seem to meet the needs of the play? Did it affect the production, and if so, how?

Scenery

1. What information was conveyed by the scenery about time, place, characters, and situation? How was this information conveyed to you?

2. What was the overall atmosphere of the setting?

3. Did any colors dominate? How did colors affect your impression of the theater event?

4. Was the setting a specific place, or was it no recognizable or real locale? Did that choice seem appropriate for the play?

5. If the setting was realistic, how effectively did it reproduce what the place would actually look like?

6. Were there symbolic elements in the scenery? If so, what were they? How did they relate to the play?

Costumes

1. What information was conveyed by the costumes about time, place, characters, and situation? How was this information conveyed to you?

2. What was the period of the costumes? What was the style? Were the costumes from a period other than the period in which the play was written or originally set? If so, how did this affect the production? Why do you think this choice was made?

3. How was color used to give you clues to the personalities of the characters?

4. Did each character's costume or costumes seem appropriate for his or her personality, social status, occupation, etc.? Why or why not?

5. Did the costumes help you understand conflicts, differing social groups, and interpersonal relationships? If so, how?

Lighting

1. What information was conveyed by the lighting about time, place, characters, and situation? How was this information conveyed to you?

2. Describe the mood of the lighting. How was color and intensity used to affect mood? What other characteristics of light were used to affect mood? Was the lighting appropriate for the mood of each scene? Why or why not?

3. Was the lighting realistic or nonrealistic? What was the direction of the light? Did it seem to come from a natural source, or was it artificial? Did this choice seem appropriate for the text?

4. Were the actors properly lit? Could their faces be seen?

5. Were light changes made slowly or quickly? How did this affect the play? Did it seem right for the play?

Text

1. What was the text for the performance? Was it a traditional play? Was it a piece created by the actors or director? ("Director's Note" on page 10 is an example of a production created by performers and director.) Was the piece improvisatory? (Note that most productions you attend will use traditional scripts as texts, and most of the following questions are based on this traditional model. However, you can adapt these questions for texts which have been created in nontraditional ways.)

2. What was the text about? What was the author of the text trying to communicate to the audience? Did the author try to communicate more than one message?

3. How was the meaning of the text communicated through words, actions, or symbols?

4. Did you agree with the point of view of the text? Why or why not?

5. What was the genre of the text? Was it comedy, tragedy, farce, melodrama, or tragicomedy? Was the text realistic or nonrealistic? Was it presentational or representational?

6. Using terms you have encountered in your theater course or textbook, describe the structure of the text. Was it climactic (intensive)? Was it episodic (extensive)? Was it some combination of the two?

7. Many theorists argue that conflict is necessary for a dramatic text. Describe the conflict within the text in the production you saw. Which characters were in conflict? Was there a moment in the action when the conflict seemed to come to a head? Was the conflict resolved or not? How did you feel about its resolution or lack of resolution? If the conflict was resolved, how was it resolved? How did the conflict seem to embody the meaning of the text?

Characters

1. What were the major desires, goals, objectives, and motivations of the leading characters? How did these help you understand the meaning of the text?

2. Were the characters realistic, symbolic, allegorical, totally divorced from reality, etc.?

3. How did minor characters relate to major characters? For instance, were they contrasts or parallels?

4. Did you identify most with one of the characters? If so, describe this character and explain why you identified with him or her.

Worksheets for Theatergoing

The following worksheets have been designed as an aid to note-taking. They should be used while you are attending a production. They do not call for extensive information; rather, they will help you jot down quick impressions that you can use later to jog your memory when you are actually developing your report. That is, the questions on these sheets are meant to help you accumulate information which can be used to respond to the more in-depth questions in the preceding section. To fill out the worksheets, you will enter information at three different times during your attendance at a theater event.

Remember: Do *not* try to write an essay or even any fully developed statements while you are watching the performance; that would defeat the whole purpose of theatergoing.

Notes before the performance

1. Theater:
   a. Jot down three adjectives which describe the atmosphere of the theater.

   b. What kind of theater is it: proscenium, thrust, arena, found space?

   c. Draw a quick sketch of the auditorium area below.

2. Program:

    a. Jot down when and where the play is set, and any other information you have gleaned from the program.

    b. Read any notes in the program and underline three sentences which you believe will help you better understand the production.

    c. Underline any historical information in the program about the play or playwright.

3. Playing space:

    a. Can you see the playing space before the performance begins?

    b. If you can see the playing space, what are your impressions about the scenery? What does it seems to suggest about the production? (Just jot down a few adjectives that reflect your first impressions.)

Intermission notes

1. Who is the central character? With whom does this character conflict? Write down their names.

2. For each of the characters you have just named, jot down three adjectives that describe his or her personality and physical attributes.

3. For each of the characters you have named, write down three adjectives to describe how you feel about the performance of the actor playing him or her.

4. Briefly describe a specific moment or scene that you thought was particularly dramatic, effective, or significant.

5. Describe a striking use of an image or simile by a character, or a moment in which such an image is used.

6. Has any character directly addressed the audience? Note who and (very briefly) when.

7. Jot down three adjectives that reflect your impressions about each of the following.

Scenery:

Costumes:

Lighting:

8. Write one word or one short phrase which best describes the world of the play (for instance, *absurd, unceasingly violent, repressed, uncontrollably cruel, sentimentally romantic, constantly hilarious*).

9. Have any audience members been asked to participate in some way? If so, describe how; also, describe your own reaction.

Notes after the performance

1. List your initial responses to each of the production elements. Indicate whether you like or dislike each element, and provide an adjective which expresses why you like or dislike it. (Remember that it is these initial responses you will have to defend in your paper.)

2. Review your intermission notes. After the intermission (or after each intermission, if there was more than one), have you changed your opinion about any of the production elements? If so, jot down what changed.

3. Write down what the high point of the action seems to have been and what resolution of the conflict, if any, has occurred.

4. Have any characters changed between the beginning and the conclusion of the action? If so, provide an adjective or a short phrase to describe the character at the outset of the action and another adjective or phrase to describe him or her after the change.

5. Does anything about the play or the production puzzle or confuse you? If so, jot it down.

6. On this basis of this experience, would you go to the theater again? Yes or no? (You will probably not include this point in your paper, but your answer may interest you for its own sake.)

Bethany Cottrell
Introduction to Theater
Illinois State University
Instructor: Timothy J. Minogue
Production: <u>Sweeney Todd</u>

Give name.

The mood of (the production) jumped

out at you from the first scene. The

crazy-haired piano player implied

darkness, as well as a type of strange,

off/beat humor found (through out) the   *You say the same thing twice.*

entire production. This zany, dark

humor remained consistent (from

beginning to end.) The costume styles

reiterated this theme besides dating the

time period. I particularly enjoyed the

attempt to keep the hairstyles of some

chorus members in the time frame of

the 1850s. The ensemble's ~~groups e~~

costumes came off as simple but realistic

for their status and time period. The
color theme varied little for the entire
cast, with a few exceptions. The
(carefully chosen) use of muted tones
restated the mood of the play. The
limited palette for most of the cast made
the main characters subtly stand out.
Small touches of red for the most of the
focal characters helped to accomplish
this too. The use of period hats ~~I felt~~
deserved ~~an~~ applause for its authenticity
alone, but the (seemingly casual use)
served a larger purpose of showing the
class and the nature of different
characters. ~~Next a look at the~~
~~individual performers.~~

Sweeney Todd's attire and makeup
quickly informed the audience of his
status and his demeanor. The rumpled,

It's your paper— no need to hedge by using "I felt."

? ?

26

muddy browns he wore in the first half

of the play and his chalky white ~~lips~~ face

offset by blood-red lips portrayed a man

on the edge—of society and ~~the edge of~~

In
sanity. The second half his crisp white

lab coat and starched black pants

showed his elevated status, but

Awkward continued with the (theme of impact) his

character needed. ~~I believe~~ this

black-on-white also set off the blood to a

better advantage.

Colloq

Mrs. Lovett's costume (hit right on) for

character portrayal too. Her filthy,

buxom disarray pointed out her

craziness and wanton ways quite nicely.

Her hair polished off this impression as

well as the words of her opening song

could, "Times is (odd.") The change in the

second half to the tacky, cleavage-

This may be "hard" (Cockney).

packed red dress implied the look taken

Colloq

on by (trash) with new money. The

symbolic indication of blood did not pass

unnoticed either. Simple touches, such

as the addition of the (ribbons) to her hair   *Why*
are
for this costume indicated a keen eye   *these*
a good
and a thoroughness for detail found   *touch ?*

throughout this production.   *Tell me.*

The attire of the beggar woman,

Anthony, and Johanna proved again the
in
painstaking ~~focus on~~ detail ~~given~~ this

production. The beggar woman's

nondescript rags gave no hint of the

former "Lucy" underneath. Anthony

appeared fresh, young, and eager in his
Describe
sailor blues. His (costume change) toward   *it.*

the end seemed natural. Johanna's

attire seemed like "peaches and cream"

and the gowns spoke of the era depicted.

However,

^ Her overall appearance ~~I feel~~ marked the one flaw in the costuming of this show. The huge wig and ~~her~~ anemic makeup (lacked the finesse) showed in the other characters. The word _horrendous_ comes to my mind.

Why? How?

The rest of the secondary cast—the Judge, Beadle, Tobias, and Pirelli—splendidly proved the quality of this presentation. Each costume stood out and sharply defined the *se* characters *whose* ~~where~~ the lack of dialogue ~~from these~~ ~~crucial supporting roles~~ might have caused them to be overlooked. These roles ~~I feel~~ were magnificently handled by the play's costumer. The absurdity of Beadle, the backward wig worn by Tobias, the clash of patterns on Pirelli, and the sophisticated, moneyed look of

You've implied this above.

the Judge added a dimension to the

production that spelled quality. This

production might be tagged as one of

I.S.U.'s finest for years to come.

Bethany —
This paper has a nice sense
of detail, especially in your
second paragraph.
Remember: Simply saying that
costumes "hit right on" or "were
magnificently handled" doesn't
tell me much. Describe them
and tell me _why_ they worked.
Why is the key word.